This book is for:

_____

from:

_____

A SLUGS & BUGS STORY

The Society of Extraordinary Raccoon Society

Secret Meeting

RANDALL GOODGAME
illustrated by Joe Sutphin

B&H kids
Nashville TN

For Livi

Welcome young raccoons!

Please, take these
SOERS balloons!

Are you tired of your
age-old raccoon flaws?

All the stealing and the sneaking
And the late-night trash-can peeking,
Picking coop locks with your
Nifty raccoon claws?

In our secretive society,
We put the pie in piety,
For we love to feast
With jolly raccoon friends.

But what *really* makes us merry
(And some say extraordinary!)
Is *how* we buck those
Naughty raccoon trends.

We give our things away!
That's right—it's quite
Shocking to say,
And quite the opposite of
What we did before.

Coats and mittens, fresh French fries,
Magic markers, pumpkin pies—
Now we give our things to those
Who need them more.

A favorite hat, a purple plum,
Even your last stick of gum—
Any kindness shared with love
Can bring good cheer.

Why do we do it? Well, it's fun!
But that's not reason number one.
The biggest reason is . . .
Well, you can read it here!

"Whoever sows sparingly
will also reap sparingly.
Whoever sows generously
will also reap generously.
Each of us should give
whatever he has decided to give,
because God loves a cheerful giver."

If you say, "That doesn't rhyme."
You'll be right most every time.
But still, there's much summed up
In those two verses.

And once you try it, you'll declare
That life is better when you share,
And learning *that* is worth much more
Than many purses.

I know how you must feel.
When I was young, I used to steal.
And sometimes still I get that
Sticky-fingered itch.

But then I sing our SOERS song,
Or maybe Luna comes along,
And I remember right from wrong
—And which is which!

Then they laughed and hugged goodbye,
And Morty said, "Thanks for the pie!"
Luna answered, "Oh, we hope you'll
come back soon!"

And when they ran into the clear,
Old Chauncey shed a happy tear
As little Maggie handed Morty
her balloon.

A generous person will be blessed.
—Proverbs 22:9